jeans

jacket

socks

cap

This Is the Baby

Candace Fleming

PICTURES BY

Maggie Smith

MELANIE KROUPA BOOKS • FARRAR, STRAUS AND GIROUX • NEW YORK

For Emily Hope and Katelyn Ann—Go for it, girls!
—C.F.

For naked babies everywhere!
—M.S.

Text copyright © 2004 by Candace Fleming
Illustrations copyright © 2004 by Maggie Smith
All rights reserved
Distributed in Canada by Douglas & McIntyre Ltd.
Color separations by Chroma Graphics PTE Ltd.
Printed and bound in the United States of America by Phoenix Color Corporation
Designed by Jennifer Browne
First edition, 2004
10 9 8 7 6 5 4 3 2 1

www.fsgkidsbooks.com

    Library of Congress Cataloging-in-Publication Data
Fleming, Candace.
    This is the baby / Candace Fleming ; pictures by Maggie Smith.— 1st ed.
        p. cm.
    Summary: A cumulative rhyme enumerating all the items of clothing that go on the
baby who hates to be dressed, from the diaper often a mess to the jacket woolen and plaid.
    ISBN 0-374-37486-4
    [1. Babies—Fiction.   2. Clothing and dress—Fiction.   3. Stories in rhyme.]   I. Smith,
Maggie, 1965– ill.   II. Title.

PZ8.3.F63775 Th 2004
[E]—dc21

                                                    2002070941

THIS IS THE BABY
who hates to be dressed.

"No! No! Nooo!"

This is the diaper, often a mess,
that goes on the baby who hates to be dressed.

"No! No! Nooo!"

This is the T-shirt,
wrinkled a lot,
that snaps over the diaper,
often a mess,

that goes on the baby who hates to be dressed.

"No!
No!
Nooo!"

This is the sweater,
  itchy and hot,
that covers the T-shirt,
  wrinkled a lot,
that snaps over the diaper,
  often a mess,
that goes on the baby
  who hates to be dressed.

"No! No! Nooo!"

These are the jeans, stiff in the knee,
that match the sweater, itchy and hot,
that covers the T-shirt, wrinkled a lot,
that snaps over the diaper, often a mess,
that goes on the baby who hates to be dressed.

"No! No! Nooo!"

These are the socks, thick as can be,
that tuck under the jeans, stiff in the knee,
that match the sweater, itchy and hot,
that covers the T-shirt, wrinkled a lot,
that snaps over the diaper, often a mess,
that goes on the baby who hates to be dressed.

"No! No! Nooo!"

These are the boots, pinchy and tight,
that fit over the socks, thick as can be,
that tuck under the jeans, stiff in the knee,
that match the sweater, itchy and hot,
that covers the T-shirt, wrinkled a lot,
that snaps over the diaper, often a mess,
that goes on the baby who hates to be dressed.

This is the cap, colored so bright,
that is worn with the boots,
   pinchy and tight,
that fit over the socks,
   thick as can be,
that tuck under the jeans,
   stiff in the knee,

that match the sweater,
  itchy and hot,
that covers the T-shirt,
  wrinkled a lot,
that snaps over the diaper,
  often a mess,
that goes on the baby
  who hates to be dressed.

Nooo!"

This is the jacket, woolen and plaid,
that goes with the cap, colored so bright,
that is worn with the boots, pinchy and tight,
that fit over the socks, thick as can be,
that tuck under the jeans, stiff in the knee,

that match the sweater, itchy and hot,
that covers the T-shirt, wrinkled a lot,
that snaps over the diaper, often a mess,
that goes on the baby who hates to be dressed.

"No! No! Nooo!"

"All done," sighs Mommy.
She looks tired but glad,
after zipping the jacket,
woolen and plaid.

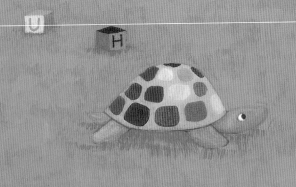

THIS IS THE BABY,
red-faced and mad,

who unzips the jacket,
woolen and plaid,

and flings off the cap,
colored so bright,

and kicks off the boots,
pinchy and tight,

and peels off the socks,
thick as can be,

and yanks off the jeans,
stiff in the knee,

and tears off the sweater,
itchy and hot,

and unsnaps the T-shirt,
wrinkled a lot,

and strips off the diaper,
often a mess,

then wiggles,

and giggles,

free and undressed.

diaper

boots

T-shirt

sweater